The Forgotten Flag

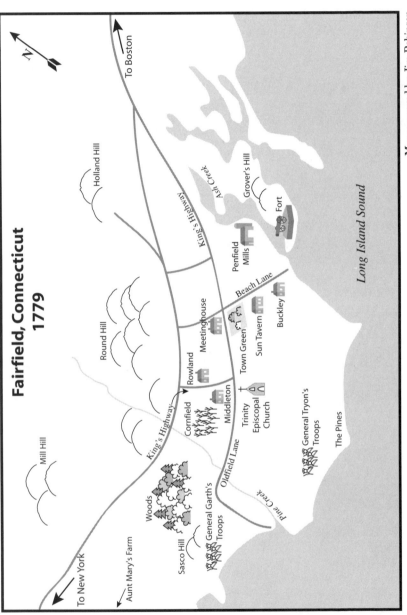

Fairfield, Connecticut 1779

N

To Boston

Holland Hill

King's Highway

Ash Creek

Grover's Hill

Fort

Penfield Mills

Beach Lane

Round Hill

Meetinghouse

Town Green

Sun Tavern

Buckley

Long Island Sound

Rowland

Mill Hill

Cornfield

Middleton

King's Highway

Trinity Episcopal Church

Oldfield Lane

General Tryon's Troops

The Pines

Woods

Sasco Hill

General Garth's Troops

Pine Creek

Aunt Mary's Farm

To New York

Map prepared by Jim Robinson

The Forgotten Flag

Revolutionary Struggle in Connecticut

by
Frances Y. Evan

WHITE MANE KIDS
SHIPPENSBURG, PENNSYLVANIA

This book is a work of historical fiction. Some names, characters, places, and incidents are products of the author's imagination and are based on actual events.

This White Mane Books publication
was printed by
Beidel Printing House, Inc.
63 West Burd Street
Shippensburg, PA 17257-0708 USA

The acid-free paper used in this book meets the guidelines for permanence and durability of the Committee on Production Guidelines for Book Longevity of the Council on Library Resources.

For a complete list of available publications
please write
White Mane Books
Division of White Mane Publishing Company, Inc.
P.O. Box 708
Shippensburg, PA 17257-0708 USA

Library of Congress Cataloging-in-Publication Data

Evan, Frances Y.
     The forgotten flag : revolutionary struggle in Connecticut / by Frances Y. Evan.
     p. cm.
     Summary: In 1779, when British and Hessian troops invade Fairfield, Connecticut, the town militia resists, resulting in a crisis for Ben and Thomas Middleton's family and their neighbors.
     ISBN 1-57249-338-0 (alk. paper)
     1. Connecticut--History--Revolution, 1775-1783--Juvenile fiction. 2. United States--History--Revolution, 1775-1783--Juvenile fiction. [1. Fairfield (Conn.)--History--18th century--Fiction. 2. Connecticut--History--Revolution, 1775-1783--Fiction. 3. United States--History--Revolution, 1775-1783--Fiction. 4. Brothers--Fiction.] I. Title.

PZ7.E8736Fo 2003
[Fic]--dc21

                                                                              2003043086

PRINTED IN THE UNITED STATES OF AMERICA

Contents

Chapter 1   The Discovery 1

Chapter 2   The Warning 5

Chapter 3   "Prepare for Attack!" 11

Chapter 4   A Town in Panic 15

Chapter 5   Round Hill 19

Chapter 6   The Hessian 21

Chapter 7   In the Cornfield 24

Chapter 8   Shots Fired 27

Chapter 9   Bloodshed 33

Chapter 10   King's Highway 39

Chapter 11   In Defiance of the Enemy 42

Chapter 12   The Pillaging of Fairfield 47

Chapter 13   The Brothers Flee 56

Chapter 14   The Pursuit 59

Chapter 15   The Hiding Place 64

Chapter 16   The Smoldering Remains 75

Chapter 17   A Patriot's Sacrifice 81

Epilogue 84

Chapter One

The Discovery

Fairfield, Connecticut, 1964

Ruth and Deborah climbed the attic stairs in the old house rather nervously. The stairs were worn and squeaked and creaked eerily with each step. The long room was very dim. Not much light penetrated the small windows at each end of the attic. Ruth clicked on the flashlight she was holding. She shone the beam around. Long timbers stretched across the ceiling and rough-hewn boards formed short knee-walls around the perimeter. There were wide planks on the floor. The room smelled musty and stale. The attic was loaded with boxes containing items to be unpacked later. The cousins were in search of a box marked "Games."

"It's really spooky up here," said Deborah, her voice echoing in the emptiness. "It is," replied Ruth a little frightened. "I haven't been up here before." The girls reached the top of the stairs and searched amongst the boxes. "Here it is!" Deborah exclaimed. "Slide these other boxes out of the way so we can open it," she said. "What games do you have?"

"Oh, let's see," Ruth replied, as she pushed boxes aside. "Life...Monopoly...Scrabble..."

One of the boxes bumped against the wall near the top of the stairs, knocking a section of board loose. It leaned back against the box, revealing a crawl space behind.

"Oops!" Ruth said surprised. Deborah approached the wall. "Wow," she said. "What's back there?"

"I don't know," Ruth replied. She slid the box and the loose board away from the opening and shone the beam of her flashlight into the space. She and Deborah peered inside. "I see something!" Deborah exclaimed. She crawled in. Something was hanging from one of the roof rafters. She tugged at it and it fell away. "What is it?" Ruth asked. Deborah crawled back to the opening where Ruth shone the light directly onto a length of soiled fabric. "It looks like a flag," said Ruth. "It's very old and dirty. Look how it's stained." Deborah held it up. The flag hung stiff and wrinkled. "Look at the stars," Deborah directed. She counted them quickly. "Thirteen...wow. What do you suppose it is doing up here?"

"Don't know," said Ruth. "Come on, let's go show it to my mother."

Ruth's mother, Vera, was in the kitchen organizing the cabinets and pantry. She adored her new home. The old house stood higher up and further back from the road than the other houses on the street. It had once been a farmhouse and dated back more than two hundred years. The dwelling had been well maintained during the previous two centuries by its various owners. The gracious colonial was painted white and had sturdy, black shutters that actually closed and latched at every window. Vera had been drawn by the character and history of the farmhouse the moment she had stepped inside. She admired the beamed ceilings and the fine craftsmanship of the original woodwork throughout the house. She loved the rustic kitchen. It still had the original fireplace with its grand, wooden mantel and brick ovens on each side.

The girls burst in holding the flag. They were both talking at once, explaining excitedly how they had found it. Vera took the flag from them and stared at it in awe.

"It must be very old, Auntie Vera," Deborah said.

"Yes, I do believe it is," Vera responded.

"Who do you suppose stuffed it in the roof rafters?" Ruth asked.

"I wish I knew. Whoever put it there did so a very long time ago."

"Look how stained it is," Deborah remarked. "I wonder why it is so stained."

"Perhaps I will take it to the Fairfield Historical Society and see if they can tell me anything about the flag," Vera replied. The young cousins nodded satisfied. They moved to the kitchen table to play their game. As they set it up they continued to chat and wonder about the flag.

Vera walked slowly to the dining room lost in thought. She opened an antique box that she kept on the hutch. There were papers stored inside it. The previous owner had passed on to her the original deed, a yellowing surveyor's map and faded photographs of the farmhouse taken in various decades. Vera laid the flag on the dining room table. She smoothed the creases gently. The fabric was brittle and stiff. Carefully she folded the old flag. How she wished she knew its story. She felt certain that it was very special. She looked at the folded cloth a moment longer wondering and then, with a sigh, she placed the forgotten flag inside the box.

Chapter Two

The Warning

Fairfield, Connecticut, July 6, 1779

Benjamin Middleton and Samuel Rowland raced across the field toward the creek. It was a good race. They were well matched. Ben was a little older and bigger than Sam and he had a longer stride. Sam was thin and wiry and light on his feet. They ran in their bare feet, laughing and puffing with the effort. Sam whooped in victory when he passed Ben just seconds before they reached the old oak tree that marked the end of the race. They leaned against the tree for a while, catching their breath. The racers were hot and sticky with sweat. The evening was hot and humid. Ben and Sam stripped off their clothes and waded into the creek. It was not very deep. The friends found a comfortable place to lie down and they relaxed with grateful sighs as the cool water flowed over them. The boys remained silent for a while, enjoying the sound of the creek gurgling over rocks. They closed their eyes, relishing this short time of freedom and idleness. Their day had been filled with chores and errands and they were happy to enjoy the company of a friend. Ben and Sam listened to birds singing in the trees, bees buzzing in the clover, a frog croaking downstream and the crickets chirping in the tall grass. The sun was low in the sky and faint streaks of pink promised a glorious sunset.

"I'll beat you next time," stated Ben. "I was slow because I twisted my ankle earlier chasing Mr. Lewis' dog out of the chicken coop."

"Oh really?" Sam replied. "Well, I spent almost all day weeding Ma's garden and chopping firewood. My back aches something awful."

"Yes, well...I'll beat you next time."

"We'll see."

They were quiet again for a while and then Sam propped himself up on an elbow and looked over at Ben. "Have you seen it again, Ben? Thomas's flag."

Ben opened his eyes and gazed up at the sky. "No," he answered. "He only showed it to me that one time." He paused, remembering. "Oh, it was beautiful, Sam. I have never seen a blue so blue before. And the stars, they stood out against the blue like the stars in the night sky, thirteen of them, one for each colony. The red and white stripes were bright and bold and...powerful."

"Where did Thomas get it?" Sam asked.

"It was a gift from Papa when he came home from the war for a while. Papa told him to look after it and to keep Mama and Abby and me safe. Thomas keeps it on his person all the time."

"Do you think he'd let *me* see it?"

"I'll ask. But Thomas is very busy. He is not home much anymore. He goes up to Round Hill to drill and train with Colonel Whiting's troops. When he does come home he is busy with the heavy work that we haven't been able to do." Ben turned to look at Sam.

"In four more years, when I'm sixteen, I'm going to train like Thomas. I'm going to learn how to use a musket and I'm going to fight the British."

"Do you think the war will last that long?" Sam asked. "Four more years."

"I don't know. Maybe."

"I'll fight too, Ben. We'll fight together," said Sam.

The boys languished in the creek a while longer as the sky changed color from pink to red then to orange. The shadows of the trees stretched long across the creek and the field. Ben and Sam stood up and waded out of the creek. They squeezed the water out of their hair and rubbed their bodies casually with their shirts. Then they dressed and walked slowly back toward town. They had not gone very far when they heard the thrumming of hoofs in the distance. They ran to the top of a hill in time to see two horsemen galloping toward Fairfield. There was purpose and urgency in the speed and manner of their gallop. The boys turned to look at each other and without a word ran back to town, following the path of the horses.

By the time Ben and Sam reached the center of town, daylight was fading and glimmers of candlelight shone inside homes as they ran past. They ran along King's Highway to the town green. They crossed the green and halted in front of The Sun Tavern. Two tired, steaming horses drank from the trough outside. The door stood ajar and the windows were open so that the boys could hear excited voices coming from inside.

"I come from New Haven. The town was attacked and burned while I was there today," a voice cried out. "I fear that Fairfield will be next! Get to your homes. Spread the word and prepare for an attack!"

"The British won't bother with Fairfield, David," someone countered. "What threat are we to them?"

"We are a thriving community. Just look at our fields, our livestock, our businesses and trade. Most of our citizens openly support independence from British rule. They wish to put us down, teach us a lesson. We must be ready." His voice rose. "To your homes, to your homes! Prepare to defend yourselves." Excited chatter followed amid the scraping of chairs and benches across the wooden floorboards. People were leaving the tavern hurrying home. A few remained behind scoffing at the notion that a British raid was imminent. George Hoyt sat by himself staring sadly into his mug of ale. He knew that there would be a raid. He had already made his plans. He would be safe.

The boys watched the departing figures fade into the twilight. Ben clutched Sam's arm. "We must get home, Sam, and I must find Thomas." Sam nodded and the boys parted, running home as the last streaks of light faded from the sky.

Ben rushed into the kitchen. Ben's sister, Abby, was lighting candles in the wall sconces. His mother was tending the iron kettle on the fire. She turned, wiping her glistening face on her apron, preparing to scold him for being late. "Where have you been, Ben?" she asked. "Did I not say be back before nightfall? Your brother is doing your work for you."

"Thomas is here?" Ben cried. "I must speak to him. I have news."

"Tell me your news then, Ben." Ben swung around as Thomas entered the kitchen from the yard, carrying two buckets of water from the well. "What is it? Did you catch any frogs at the creek today? Shall we add them to Mama's stew pot?" Thomas teased.

"The British raided New Haven today!" Ben exclaimed. "David Hall believes that Fairfield will be next." Thomas placed the heavy buckets on the floor and took hold of Ben's shoulders. He looked directly into his eyes. "Where did you hear this, Ben?"

"At the tavern. Sam and I were at the creek. We heard riders. We followed them to the tavern and heard David Hall warn of a raid." Thomas released Ben's shoulders and turned to his mother. "We were afraid of this. The British are increasing their raids. It seems they intend to attack towns along the Connecticut shoreline to demoralize us and teach us a lesson for supporting the cause for independence." Thomas picked up his leather pouch from the table. He slung the long strap over his head and thrust one arm through. He reached for his hat and his musket. "Mama, I must go. I've got to get back to Round Hill. No doubt Colonel Whiting has been informed and is preparing for the raid even now." Abby blew out her taper and stared at Thomas with wide, frightened eyes. She began to cry. "Thomas, please don't go. I'm afraid." Sarah Middleton went to her daughter and hugged her to her side. Thomas approached them quickly and squatted before Abby. "Now Abby, be brave. I will be close by." Thomas stood and looked at his mother. "If the British come, go immediately to

Aunt Mary's. The farm is far enough away from town that the British won't bother with it." Sarah's eyes were bright with unshed tears. She raised her hand and gently touched Thomas's cheek. "Take care, Thomas. God save you." Thomas kissed her quickly, then turned and strode toward the door. "Thomas," Ben called to him. "Do you have the flag?" Thomas turned and smiled at Ben. He patted his leather pouch. "Always, Ben. Always." And then he was gone.

Chapter Three

 "Prepare for Attack!"

July 7, 1779

Ben woke with a start. The cannon had fired at the fort on Grover's Hill. Ben pulled off his nightshirt and fumbled for his clothes. It was still dark outside and he had to feel his way across the room to the hallway. His mother was hurrying down the hall with a candle and Abby was calling out to them in a panicked voice. "Mama, Ben, what is it? I heard the cannon. Are they coming already? Are the British here?" Ben turned to the stairs. "I'll find out what's going on, Mama. You go to Abby." In the kitchen Ben lit a taper from the embers in the fireplace and then lit the lantern. He carried it outside. Town folk were gathering in the street. They called to each other. "What is it? Does anybody know?" There was nervous, excited chatter and then a group organized to investigate. They headed toward the shoreline. Ben hurried along with them.

The sky was still dark when Ben arrived at the beach. He walked down to the tide line and let the seawater wash over his bare feet. A gentle sea breeze blew into his face. He looked out to sea. In the distance he saw lights slowly swaying with the movement of the waves. He could just make out the outline of a small flotilla of ships. Ben turned to look at the others. They were standing in the sand staring and pointing out to sea and speaking nervously. He walked back up the beach and sat in the sand, placing his lantern beside him. He would wait until dawn.

Slowly the eastern sky lightened until the ships were clearly silhouetted against the sky and the sea. British flags waved lazily from the masthead in the gentle sea breeze. It appeared that the fleet was sailing slowly in the direction of New York. As everyone watched its slow progress, a haze began to form across the water. The fog thickened until the ships were completely hidden from view. The town folk stood there anxiously staring into the gray murkiness sharing their hopes and fears for Fairfield. "They are passing us by," someone called out. "The ships are sailing for New York."

"Nay!" answered another. "They raided New Haven yesterday. We will be next."

"They will come," cried David Hall. "Be ready, good people, and do all you can to protect yourselves and our good town. I must rejoin the militia. The time has come to make our stand. God be with you all."

"God protect you, David," someone shouted as the group dispersed and hurried back to town. Ben was ahead of them all, running swiftly, his lantern lying forgotten in the sand. Only George Hoyt remained on the beach. He watched the town folk depart and then he turned and walked along the shore toward the "Pines" where he would wait.

Ben found his mother gathering eggs from the chicken coop. Abby was scattering seed for the chickens. Sarah swung around anxiously when she heard him rushing into the yard. He was panting with excitement and exertion as he cried out to her: "British ships off shore...sailing toward New York! But David Hall says to prepare...prepare for attack!"

Sarah's face sagged with sadness for but a moment and then it became firm with determination and resolve. Abby stood frozen staring wide-eyed at her brother. "I want you to take Abby to Aunt Mary's, Ben. I'm going to stay here."

"But Mama...no. We must all go," Ben answered, surprised. Sarah walked to Ben and smiled into his face. He was almost as tall as she. His blue eyes were bright with concern. His face was glowing and pink from his run and his light brown hair was in disarray, escaping from the cord that bound it at his neck. "I am staying, Ben. Some of the other women are staying too."

"But, Mama. Why are you staying? What can you do?"

"We will appeal to the British officers, Ben. We have heard that they conduct themselves with the utmost civility. We do not believe that they will harm us or destroy our houses and belongings if we plead for compassion and mercy."

"No. No, Mama."

"Ben. I must do this. I must try. Hurry now. Ben, Abby, gather some of your things together and be on your way. Tell Aunt Mary what has happened. The farm should be safe, but tell her to be alert and ready, just in case."

Ben made no more protestations. His mother's mind was made up. He would take care of Abby. He would get her safely to Aunt Mary's farm. But he would return. He would hide somewhere nearby in case Thomas or his mother needed his help.

Chapter Four

 A Town in Panic

Aunt Mary had a busy household. Her husband, Matthew, was away fighting in the war, but Uncle Matthew's grandfather, old Ned, managed the farm with the help of two strong, young farmhands who helped out several days a week. Aunt Mary had a baby and three other children to care for. Ben knew that Abby loved spending time with her little cousins. She would be happily occupied and her help would be appreciated. Ben accompanied Abby to the farm and sat down long enough to gulp some cider and eat some bread and cheese. He made hurried explanations to Aunt Mary and old Ned and then jumped up to leave. "No, Ben," Aunt Mary said, tugging at his sleeve. "You must stay here at the farm." Old Ned stood up from his chair. He was rather tall and lean but sturdy and still quite strong. His face and arms were tanned brown from the hours spent outside in the sun. His hair was balding and gray but his eyes were bright as he smiled down at Ben. "If I were a younger man, I'd go with you, Ben," he said. "Do what you need to do, son. We will take care of Abby." Aunt

15

Mary began to protest. "It's alright, Mary," he said, laying a hand on her shoulder. "Take care of your mother, Ben. God be with you." Ben nodded gratefully and ran from the house. Abby tearfully watched as he sped across the field. Old Ned watched him too. "Such a brave young man, Mary," he sighed. "Such perilous times. I wish I could do something to help. I wish I could fight in the war...make myself useful." Mary looked at him in amazement. *"Make yourself useful!"* she said. "Whatever would I do without you?"

The sun had burned off the fog by the time Ben returned to the beach. He looked out across the sparkling water. He gasped. The ships were there! They were at anchor. Ben waited and watched them for a while. All was quiet. There was no activity. Several town folk made a quick appearance, checked on the ships and then hastened back to town. Ben headed to town also. He would hide in his mother's cornfield and keep a watchful eye on the house. He knew that Thomas and the militia would be somewhere close by too.

The town was busy. Families were making their preparations. Most chose to leave until the danger had passed. They were packing up their valuables and carrying them to the hills and woodland away from town. The more well-to-do were loading their wagons and carriages, preparing to travel inland. William Wheeler and his father were driving their livestock toward Toilsome Hill to keep them safe. People were calling to each other. "Are the ships there still?"

"Aye, they are at anchor."

"Are the British coming?"

"Nay. Not yet."

There had never been such a frenzy of activity in Fairfield before. Town folk were rushing to and fro carrying packs and bags, heading out of town as horse-drawn wagons and carts and carriages rumbled by raising a choking dust on the road.

As Ben passed Isaac Burr's house, he stopped in his tracks, astonished. The gentleman watchmaker was climbing into his well. He disappeared from sight for a good while and then reappeared. He clambered clumsily over the side and stood slapping at his coat and breeches to remove the dirt and dust they had accumulated. He looked up to see Ben gaping at him. He nodded and smiled. "Well, young Ben," he said. "Let the plundering fiends find my customers' watches down *there!*" Ben smiled back and waved as he continued on.

As Ben drew nearer to home he spotted Sam running ahead of him. "Sam!" he called. Sam stopped and turned, waiting until Ben caught up with him. "Have you heard, Sam? British ships. Just off the coast."

"Of course, I've heard. The whole town knows. My house is in an uproar. Everybody is running around packing things up. We are going to flee for the hills at the first sighting of troops landing. I'm going to the church. I'm going to watch from the steeple. Come with me, Ben."

"Nay. My mother sent me to Aunt Mary's farm with Abby. I took Abby there but I've come back. Mama is staying behind. She hopes to save our house. I want to be close by in case she needs me. I'll hide in the cornfield." Sam smiled at Ben in admiration. "God be with you, Ben."

"And with you, Sam." Sam turned and continued running toward the church. Ben left the road well before he reached his house lest his mother see him and send him away again. He kept to the long grass until he reached his mother's cornfield. He sat just inside the edge nearest the house where he could peer through the stalks and keep watch.

Chapter Five

Round Hill

Thomas was pacing on Round Hill. He was restless and tense with nervous energy and anticipation. He was soon going to experience his first action of the war. His duty was to defend his town and its inhabitants. He was ready. He would do all that was asked of him. He would make his family proud. He thought of his mother and Ben and Abby. By now, he hoped, they would be at Aunt Mary's. They should be safe there. The recent British raids along the Connecticut shoreline targeted well-established and prosperous towns. The British probably would not venture far inland. Thomas thought of his father. He prayed that he was safe wherever he may be. There had been few letters over the last three years and even fewer visits from him. The last time Thomas had seen him he had given him the flag. "This is what I fight for, Tom," he had said. "Take care of this for me. I entrust it to you. The time may come when you too have to fight. Keep it with you. It will give you fortitude and courage." He had laughed then and slapped Thomas on the back. "In the meantime, son, you must keep this place going for me. Take care of your mother and brother and sister so that I have my home and family to come back to." Thomas patted his leather pouch. The flag was neatly folded inside. Well, the time had come for him to fight, for freedom, for his family and his home. He would make them all proud.

Thomas observed the militiamen as they gathered. There were men from Fairfield and men from neighboring towns. The militia included farmers, millers, blacksmiths, carpenters, clockmakers, wheelwrights, tinsmiths, shoemakers, shop and tavern owners and many other tradesmen. Some slaves too, with the permission of their owners, joined the ranks. All left their work and took up arms to stand together against British oppression. Colonel Whiting was the commanding officer. He received reports as militiamen arrived from town and country. He discussed plans and strategy with other leaders and he rallied the troops with short speeches of encouragement and bravado. Thomas thought the colonel was a good leader and was anxious to prove himself.

The waiting, though, was difficult. The British ships were at anchor. When would they come ashore? When would the action begin? Thomas was ready. He had checked his weapon. It was clean and in good working order. His cartridge box was full and dry and his axe hung newly sharpened from his belt. His leather pouch carried extra flints, tinderbox and a jack knife. He sat for a while in the grass with some of his young comrades. There was a game going on. Someone had pounded musket balls into cube shapes and marked them up as dice. Thomas was invited to play. He joined in for a time but soon left them to their game. He could not sit still. He paced.

Chapter Six

 **The Hessian**

On the British ship *Camilla*, anchored in Long Island Sound off the Fairfield coastline, another young man paced. Friedrich was ready too. Friedrich was a Hessian soldier. He was part of a German contingent hired by the British to increase their numbers and ensure the defeat of the rebel Americans. Yesterday's raid of New Haven had been very unsuccessful. A large militia had forced a retreat before the troops had been able to burn or pillage much at all. The militia had used heavy cannon fire against them too. Friedrich had been surprised and angry by the defeat and he was eager to settle the score.

He sat down beside Karl with a frustrated grunt. He spoke in German to his friend.

"What are we waiting for, Karl? All this idleness disturbs me. I am anxious to teach these peasants a lesson."

"Be patient, my friend," Karl replied. "We will be on our way soon enough. I am sure that General Tryon and General Garth have their reasons for waiting. And I hear tell that the wait will be worthwhile. There are some wealthy homes in this town of Fairfield. There should be some good pickings to add to our spoils."

"Ah, yes. That is good, Karl. We will return to Germany as rich men, eh?" Friedrich slapped Karl on the back with a hearty laugh. Karl smiled and stared dreamily out at the water. "It will be good to go home, Friedrich. We have been gone overlong. How could we have known it would take these long years to put down the rebels? How is it that they continue to oppose us with such strength and persistence?"

"Karl, they cannot succeed," Friedrich answered with indignation. "These untrained, undisciplined peasants and farmers cannot last against our sophisticated forces and the might of the British military."

"Ah, Friedrich. But their numbers grow and they fight with strong resolve." Karl paused and turned to his friend. "Do you not think of the cool mountains and vast forests of our homeland, Friedrich? I think of the fields of heather and the lakes and rivers. I yearn for my town. I would like to build a fine house. It is time for a wife and children and..."

"*Ach!* You have gone soft, Karl," Friedrich mocked. "We have much to do here before we can think about such things." Friedrich rose and paced again. "And I am most keen to be at it, Karl. Most keen."

Isaac Jarvis, up on Grover's Hill looked through his spyglass toward the British ships. He knew the troops would soon disembark. He was waiting with twenty-six men. They would do everything they could at their little fort to deter the enemy. They had a twelve-pounder cannon that could hit a target with a good degree of accuracy almost one thousand yards away. Its maximum range was three thousand yards. They were well armed with cannon ball and grapeshot. And, if the British tried to attack the fort, the brave men, armed with their muskets, would defend it with their lives.

Chapter Seven

In the Cornfield

The warm day wore on. Ben sat uncomfortably in the cornfield swatting at flies and mosquitoes, waiting. He watched people hurrying down the road throughout the morning and afternoon. They carried bundles and pulled carts loaded with possessions. His mother would appear from time to time. She was going about her usual chores but stopped to speak to her neighbors as they left. "Come away with us, Sarah!" they said. "'Tis not safe to linger overlong." But Sarah shook her head. "Some of the women have decided to stay. I am staying too. We will plead for our homes and our livelihoods."

The neighbors nodded dubiously and wished her God's blessing and protection and continued on their way. Sarah watched them go, waving until they disappeared from sight.

It occurred to Ben in the cornfield that should he need to protect his mother, he was without a weapon. He noticed the large axe behind the house. It was leaning against a tree stump where it was used for chopping firewood. He waited until his mother went back inside the house and then he sprang out of the cornfield, ran across the dusty yard and seized the axe. He dashed back and hid again amongst the cornstalks. He felt better.

Ben waited. He wondered what was happening. When were the British coming ashore? Perhaps they would not after all. Perhaps they would sail on up the coast or return to Long Island. Waiting and wondering was hard. Ben was restless and nervous with anticipation. He was worried about his mother and the other women who had decided to stay behind. He was worried about his brother, Thomas, and the battle ahead. He was worried about his beloved town and everything that was dear and familiar. He was worried about his father and whether he would return when the war was over. It was rather distressing waiting and worrying in the cornfield. He also realized he was very hungry.

Ben saw his mother come out of the house into the yard. She was carrying a small bundle. He watched her take a shovel from the storehouse. She measured off several paces from the corner of the chicken coop and dug a shallow hole. Sarah placed the bundle in the hole and stood staring down at it for a moment or two. Then she dropped the shovel and tugged at her finger. She bent down to place her wedding ring with the bundle, then picked up the shovel and filled in the hole. She returned the shovel to the storehouse and hurried back inside. Ben was filled with admiration for his mother. She was determined to keep some of the family's valuables hidden from the enemy. Observing this simple act brought the full impact of the threat and danger they all faced to a new reality for Ben. He gripped the axe handle defiantly.

Chapter Eight

Shots Fired

George Hoyt was in place on the beach. The time was getting close now. Soon the troops would be disembarking the ships into the flat boats that would bring them to shore. George knew that most of the townsfolk would despise him for what he was about to do, but it was a matter of survival. He had General Tryon's word that his sister's home would not be touched. Nor would the homes of other family members. And they would all be safe and not harmed in any way. George was confident that he was doing the right thing. He looked out across the water, observing the ships at anchor. He thought he detected some activity. Yes. He saw the boats being lowered over the side of the gunships. They were on their way. He watched the boats draw nearer and nearer to the beach with feelings of resignation and dread. He took a deep breath. He was ready to perform his duty. Although he was at peace with his decision, he took no pleasure in the deed.

The boats carried the flank companies of the Guard, part of the Hessian Landgraf Regiment and the King's American Regiment led by General Tryon. There were also artillerymen and two field pieces of cannon. George shook his head sadly as his saw the large number of soldiers in the boats. Fairfield did not stand a chance. On the beach the troops disembarked and the flat boats returned to the ships to bring the remaining troops of Hessians led by General Garth to shore. They would come ashore a mile further west and march over Sasco Hill into town. George greeted General Tryon and then he strode ahead guiding the troops along the beach. He led them to Beach Lane, where he turned, and they followed him toward the center of town. The troops marched in neat rows, their muskets on their shoulders and uniform colors bright in the sunshine. The British wore the familiar red coat with elaborate facings over white shirt and breeches. They wore black boots and tall black hats. The Hessians wore a similar uniform but the coat was blue.

From the steeple of the Episcopal Church on the west side of town, Samuel Rowland watched the advancing troops in fear and dread. He spun around and clambered down the steeple stairs in a panic. He ran down the center aisle of the church and burst out of the front door. He ran toward home, stopping briefly at Ben's cornfield. He darted into the field, pushing aside the cornstalks and calling to his friend. "Ben...Ben," he called in breathless gasps. "The British have landed. They are marching up Beach Lane even now."

"I'm here, Sam," Ben replied, moving in the direction of Sam's voice. "There are lots of them, Ben, two field pieces too. They..." Sam paused at the sound of cannon fire. "The cannon at Grover's Hill," said Ben. "It must be firing at the troops."

"That should slow them down a bit," Sam grinned. "I'd better get home, Ben. God keep you."

"God keep you, Sam."

Sam turned and pushed his way through the cornstalks again toward the edge. He called back to Ben from the road. "Ben, does Thomas have the flag with him?"

"Yes, Sam. He does."

"I'm glad." And then Sam was gone, running desperately for home.

The troops had not progressed far along Beach Lane when the cannon on Grover's Hill began to fire. It fired both grapeshot and ball. The officers shouted orders as the grapeshot exploded above them and cannon balls raised huge clouds of dust upon impact. Then, while the troops were dealing with the cannon fire, the militia began to fire on the troops. The militia had taken up positions behind the stone walls along the road. The British halted in their advance. Orders were shouted and they returned fire. The skirmish was short. The large numbers of British troops prevailed, but not without casualties. A soldier staggered and fell, clutching his chest as blood gushed through his fingers. Another screamed as grapeshot tore away an ear. Cannon balls forced the enemy to break formation and dive for cover. There were shouts and moans with each impact.

Thomas hunched low behind the wall. He was fighting his first battle. He reloaded his musket, performing the steps smoothly and rapidly as he had practiced so many times before. He half cocked the firelock and withdrew a cartridge from his cartridge box. He bit off the top and shook a portion of the powder into the pan. He shut the pan and emptied the remaining powder from the cartridge and the ball into the barrel of his musket. He drew the ramrod, rammed the cartridge down the barrel and replaced it. He cocked the firelock and was ready to fire. As he accomplished the steps, he listened in awe to the sounds of aggression around him. There was the booming of the cannon, the cracking of muskets, the shouts of officers and the cries and moans of the injured, sounds that were out of place in the little town of Fairfield.

Thomas positioned himself on one knee and brought the musket to his shoulder. He slowly rose up to peer over the stone wall. The enemy troops were in disarray, no longer in their marching formation. Some of the troops were heading toward the walls, their muskets pointing forward and bayonets flashing in the sun. One British soldier was approaching the wall not far from Thomas's location. Thomas aimed at the soldier and pulled the trigger. The musket ball tore into the soldier's leg, shredding his breeches and exposing mutilated flesh. The soldier screamed and dropped to the ground, crawled to the stone wall for cover and grabbed at his wound in agony. Several British soldiers were rushing toward him. Thomas knew that he did not have time to reload his musket before the soldiers would be upon him. He stood and ran from his position. He ran along the stone wall toward town ahead of the advancing troops. As Thomas ran he heard cannon fire coming from the British gunboats. They had begun to fire on the little fort at Grover's Hill. The cannon at the fort had to turn its fire away from the British troops and onto the gunboats. The British were able to concentrate their efforts now on the sniping militia and force them to fall back. General Tryon ordered the troops back into formation and they continued their march into town.

The British troops assembled on the town green at the top of Beach Lane. Thomas crouched in some long grass on a nearby hillside to look back at the scene. He saw someone speaking with the British general. It was George Hoyt! He had seen Hoyt leading the troops up Beach Lane. He was filled with loathing. This cowardly and selfish man, member of a prosperous Fairfield family, had made it easy for the British. He must have met them on the beach and led them through the marshes to the little road that brought them directly to the center of town. Now he was leading the general and some officers toward the Buckley house where a woman stood waiting in the doorway. Thomas scowled in disgust, then turned and ran the rest of the way to Round Hill where the militia would regroup with Colonel Whiting.

George Hoyt made nervous introductions. "General Tryon, may I introduce my sister, Mrs. Jonathan Buckley." Tryon nodded curtly. Mrs. Buckley responded with exaggerated overtures of hospitality. "General Tryon, *please* make yourself comfortable in my humble home. Whatever you want...whatever you need, just let me know. We are at your disposal." She glanced quickly at George and gave him a weak smile. "Yes, yes, my good woman," Tryon replied as he strode past her and into the house followed by his officers.

"My officers and I require refreshments and wash basins to rid ourselves of this infernal road dust."

"Of course, of course," Mrs. Buckley agreed. She watched in dismay for a moment as heavy boots clomped across her polished wooden floor. Dust rose in the beams of sunlight shining through the windows as soldiers slapped at their dusty uniforms. They were seating themselves at her fine dining room table spreading papers across the top. Buckles and sword hilts dragged across the costly furniture. She turned and hurried to the kitchen where her servants awaited her instructions.

Chapter Nine

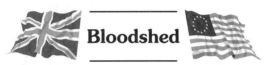

Bloodshed

The militia on Round Hill was slowly growing. Men arrived in ones and twos, eager to join the rebel force. Colonel Whiting was pleased. Although the number remained at a distinct disadvantage compared to the British contingent, he believed the militia could thwart the British in any attempt they may make to progress from the center of town. He instructed his officers to assemble the men. He wished to address them before commencing a counterattack.

"My friends and brave men of Fairfield, neighbors and comrades in arms, the time is upon us to make our stand. We may be weaker in numbers...but, men, we are stronger in our *resolve*. We shall accomplish much this day. We shall hamper the British at every turn. We shall show them that we will *not* stand idly by and yield to their oppressive might. They will know that as they dare tread upon our town, our 'fair field,' with evil intent, that the heart and spirit of a proud new nation raises up against them. Whatever the cost today we are prepared to deliver this message. We shall resist! We shall be strong! We shall be free! May God be with you lads, today and always."

The militia replied with loud cheers and shouted back words of support and confirmation. Officers then organized the soldiers into three groups. One group would move field pieces into position and defend the bridge that crossed Ash Creek, allowing access to the fort. Another group would return to the town center and take up positions to fire on the British force. The last group would remain at Round Hill to defend it from the British and prevent them from pushing inland to threaten other communities.

Thomas was assigned to the group returning to the town center under the command of Captain Nash. He left Round Hill with his musket loaded and ready. It was going to be a quick strike. Captain Nash had instructed, "On my order, men...rise, fire, load and fire, and then run." Thomas and his comrades descended the hill in a hurried, rhythmic gait. They approached the town, staying low to the ground. Near the meetinghouse they hid in tall grass behind the fence and awaited Nash's order. Thomas's face hardened in anger as he peered through the grass and observed the scene before him. On the town green the British troops stood at attention as General Tryon read aloud a proclamation to a scattering of townsfolk who had remained in town and who had gathered to listen to the British demands. Thomas did not hear all that was said but he caught enough words and phrases to understand its meaning. "...Citizens of Fairfield...allegiance to his majesty, King George... delusion in hoping for independence...voluntary submission...folly and obstinacy..." The proclamation was nailed to a post on the green. General Tryon addressed the assembled troops briefly and then he turned and strode back to the Buckley residence accompanied by his officers.

Angrily Thomas watched Tryon's arrogant departing stride as the troops on the green organized into smaller divisions. His ears were alert for Nash's signal. He was itching to give the British his response to their demand for allegiance to King George. A division stepped off the green into the street to move to another position. Thomas heard Nash's cry, "Now, lads. FIRE!" Thomas knelt on one knee, brought his musket to his shoulder and fired into the marching lines. A volley of musket fire burst amid the British lines. The British were caught completely off guard. A couple of soldiers went down. Thomas hurriedly reloaded and fired again at the disrupted formation. Muskets cracked again. Thomas saw more soldiers drop and then he heard Nash shout. "Well done, lads! Now run...*run!*" The British were firing back. Thomas turned on his heels, hunched low and fled, running quickly and nimbly over the familiar terrain. The militia retreated to Round Hill. Only one man was lost, lying sprawled and face down on the land that he loved.

The British pursued the militia to Round Hill, but the force that had remained there was in position and waiting for them. Musket fire commenced as soon as the British were in range. The British soldiers were unfamiliar with the land. The militia had them covered from hillocks and valleys, shrubs and trees as they approached. British officers soon realized the folly of attempting to take the hill. They called a retreat, and frustrated, indignant soldiers halted, turned and marched dejectedly away.

The men on the hill allowed themselves a brief, subdued celebration. They had achieved a minor victory. As the troops departed, Thomas looked down toward the town. There was smoke rising from a few chimneys, indicating that some hearth fires were still being tended. Lovely houses stood proudly in yards with gardens and flowers and herbs and hedges. Green pastures spread out from the center of town dotted with grazing animals. There were neat fields with their crops in straight rows on some of the larger properties. All was lush and green and beautiful. Thomas had never before been so aware of the beauty of Fairfield.

At Ash Creek there was a small victory also. Colonel Whiting had instructed the men to defend the bridge to prevent the British from attacking the fort and from marching into Stratfield and Stratford. The militia had overturned two heavy carts on the bridge to form a blockade. The carts had been laden with sacks of flour from nearby Penfield Mills. James Penfield had rushed to offer his help when he had seen the militia arrive at the bridge. Some of the men were on the bridge positioned behind the carts. Some were waiting in the tall reeds along the riverbank. Some were on the far side of the creek manning the field pieces.

David Hall was among those crouched behind the upturned carts. He stared ahead watching for a flash of red or the sound of marching boots on the road. He was anxious and eager for battle and to do his small part in the rebellion against oppression, arrogance and tyranny. He heard the enemy before he saw them. The rhythmic drumming of boots became louder and louder and then the red columns appeared around a curve in the road. The field pieces boomed behind David and grapeshot tore into the British troops. Orders were shouted and soldiers scattered from the road into the reeds and shrubs alongside. They continued their advance, muskets held in front of them, with bayonets flashing in the sun. David Hall took aim at one of the approaching red coats. He pulled the trigger. The musket ball found its mark. The British soldier dropped abruptly to his knees and fell facedown in the grass. David hunched down behind the wagon to reload. The field pieces fired again. David heard screams and shouts, closer now. He raised himself up again. The red coats were almost upon them, too close for the field pieces to fire again. He aimed, fired and saw an enemy soldier spin around with the impact, grabbing at his neck. He fell without a sound. No time to reload now. The British were on the bridge. Muskets cracked all around. Some of the enemy were scrambling to climb the wagon barricade. David rose up to peer over the top and found himself eyeball to eyeball with a British soldier. The soldier raised his bayonet, preparing to drive it into David's skull, but a musket cracked from somewhere behind him and the soldier was blown off the wagon and fell from sight. Another British soldier appeared. David drew his sword. Dodging the lunging bayonet, David grabbed the soldier's arm and yanked him over the barricade onto the rough boards of the bridge. He seized the musket and stabbed the soldier with his own bayonet. The battle continued. It was bloody, but short. The small British force sent by Tryon to take control of the bridge could not overpower the militia that had been lying in wait and itching for a fight. An officer shouted orders and the red coats fell back. They formed into their columns and marched away to report their failure to the general, leaving several of their comrades sprawled where they had fallen.

Chapter Ten

King's Highway

The afternoon sun was beginning its descent as evening approached. Ben had spent hours in the cornfield. He had heard sounds of battle and seen his mother emerge from the house several times to peer anxiously down King's Highway. Some of the other women who had decided to stay arrived at Sarah's house. Sarah joined them outside where they stood speaking earnestly together. Ben could not hear what was said but they were obviously nervous and worried. Together they hurried away, rushing down the road toward the center of town.

Ben hesitated, wondering if he should follow, when he became aware of a sound. It was muffled at first and then grew steadily louder. It was troops on the march. Ben hurried through the cornstalks to the side of the field that faced the road. He carefully parted the cornstalks until he could see. Approaching from the west were the soldiers under the command of General Garth. There were so many! Red coats flashed past him as he hid amongst the corn. Soldiers in blue uniform coats also. They must be

Hessians, Ben thought. He had heard of them. They were German soldiers paid by the British to fight for their cause. Ben stared in dismay as the troops marched by. He knew that little could be done against such a force. He fully realized the gravity of the situation. His home, his town and his very life were in peril. Ben waited in the cornfield for a short time after the troops had passed by and then he followed behind, staying out of sight as best as he could.

Friedrich and Karl marched past the cornfield and past Sarah Middleton's house. Their eyes swept over the lush fields and the neat homesteads as they made their way to the town center. Friedrich gave Karl a sidelong glance and quick smile as he nodded toward some of the grander houses. Karl nodded in silent approval. It would be a prosperous raid in this town of Fairfield.

When General Garth arrived at the town green, he found General Tryon angry and frustrated. British soldiers were burying their fallen comrades in shallow graves on the grounds of the meetinghouse. Fairfield's militia was posing more of a problem to the general's plans than he had expected. Outposts had been established around the center of town while he was waiting for Garth and his troops. General Tryon escorted Garth to the Buckley house to advise him of the day's events and to discuss their course of action. Tryon impatiently demanded food and drink from the ever-obliging Mrs. Buckley and her brother, George Hoyt.

The militia steadily grew in size on Round Hill. Though the British force still vastly outnumbered it, the courage and determination on the faces of the men was evident. Thomas felt proud to be one of their number. He sat on the hillside overlooking the town. He opened his leather pouch and removed the neatly folded flag. He just held it in his hands and gazed down at it. It was the symbol of everything for which they were fighting. It was a cherished gift from his father. He closed his eyes and said a quick, silent prayer. He prayed that his family would one day live in peace and happiness again and that his father would return from the war, healthy and unharmed.

Thomas opened his eyes and gazed down at the town. A haze of smoke appeared above the treetops near the town center. He shouted an alarm. Others had seen it too. Men were shouting and running and staring in dismay. As Thomas watched, the smoke thickened and became darker. Colonel Whiting stood with the men. "The British are setting fires to our homes, men. They think to frighten us into submission." There were more shouts as smoke rose from a location further to the east of town. And then more smoke at a third location, somewhere on King's Highway. The men became quiet as they watched in deepening horror. Colonel Whiting's voice boomed into the silence. "To arms, men...for, liberty, for independence, for Fairfield!"

Chapter Eleven

 In Defiance of the Enemy

General Tryon and General Garth stood on the town green with some of the troops watching the fires. Tryon had selected several homes at random and ordered them to be burned. Burning parties of several men had entered each home with flaming torches. They had set fire to the houses from the inside. The men on Grover's Hill at the fort looked down in dismay. They saw the flames first through the windows. After a few minutes the buildings exploded into fire.

"'Tis a fine town, is it not, General Garth? I would find it most regrettable to have to destroy it. Perhaps when the citizens see these few houses demolished they will come to their senses."

"'Tis fine indeed," replied Garth. "But these brief raids along the shoreline have not yet succeeded in turning the people from the folly of their struggle for independence. They are proving to be a stubborn breed."

"That they are, General. But they *will* swear allegiance to the crown or see their town reduced to ashes!" Tryon looked over at a small group of townsfolk who were gathering on the edge of the green. They were mostly women. Reverend Sayre of the Episcopal Church stood at some distance from them holding a white flag. They were all staring in horror and anguish at the fires. Tryon strode over to the group. "This is just a small example of what will become of your beloved town if you and the rest of the inhabitants will not obey the terms of the proclamation I have delivered to you this day," he declared.

Reverend Sayre stepped forward. "I am Reverend Sayre, missionary and representative of the Church of England and loyal to the King. I beseech you, in the name of God, to cease this unholy enterprise and leave these good people to their homes and peaceful lives." Sarah walked boldly toward the general, stretching an arm out toward him. Ben took a sharp intake of breath and tensed in his hiding place behind the meetinghouse. "Please, sir, do not destroy our town. We are humble folk who work hard to provide happy homes for our families and children. Please...we beseech you, do not demolish so casually all that we have so proudly built with years of toil and sacrifice and devotion." The other women added their pleas, weeping and reaching out to the general for mercy.

General Tryon responded impatiently: "My good woman, it gives me no pleasure to destroy the homes and lives of hard-working, god-fearing people. You citizens of Fairfield have only to swear your allegiance to the King and lay down your arms against us and we will do you no harm. Have *done* with your rebellion and stubbornness!" General Tryon turned from Sarah and spoke to Reverend Sayre. "I have penned a dispatch which I need delivered to the commander of the rebel force. You, good Reverend, will deliver the message." Tryon signaled one of his officers who stepped forward, extending the dispatch to the Reverend. Reverend Sayre hesitated. His loyalties were mixed. His allegiance was to England and the King but he lived amongst the people of Fairfield with his family. He knew the people intimately. He ministered to them and cared for them. He glanced back quickly at the women, then bowed his head sadly and reached out to accept the dispatch. He turned and hurried toward Round Hill. Tryon addressed the women: "Go back to your homes. Pray that the commander of your rebels displays wisdom and prudence in his response." He turned abruptly and strode back to General Garth. They conferred for a moment and then made their way back to the Buckley house. The women held on to each other's hands and wiped away tears. They returned to their homes, fearful and despairing. They knew what Colonel Whiting's answer would be.

Ben followed at a safe distance. He saw his mother enter the house. He circled around again and returned to the cornfield. He could see and smell the smoke rising in the air and spreading over the town. Surely his mother would leave now, he thought. He waited. He hoped that he would see her emerge, perhaps carrying a bag or two to make her way to Aunt Mary's. He watched. He waited. After some time, Ben realized that his mother was not going to leave.

Thomas was making his way from Round Hill toward the west end of town. His unit's mission was to protect the remaining inhabitants and to hinder the British as much as possible. Thomas was anxious to be in the vicinity of his own home. He would do whatever he could to save it.

On Round Hill, Reverend Sayre arrived with the dispatch from General Tryon. He called out as he approached, "I bring a message for Colonel Whiting from General Tryon." The militia in their positions on the hill glared at the Reverend. Many of them recognized him and shouted jeers. "Well, look at this. It's the good Reverend...carrying a missive from the King!" Reverend Sayre stopped and looked around at the men. He was taken aback by the openly hostile stares. They were the stares of men who had looked up at him with honor and respect every Sunday. He opened his mouth to speak, but Colonel Whiting was suddenly before him. "Well, Reverend," he said. "I understand you have a message for me." Reverend Sayre extended his arm and handed the dispatch to Colonel Whiting. "I beg you to submit to the demands of General Tryon, Colonel. You will cause unbearable grief and destruction if you do not. There is no use resisting. You are outnumbered. Submit and the general will be merciful." Colonel Whiting shot the reverend a look of contempt and snatched the dispatch from him. He scanned it quickly. "This dispatch contains the proclamation that was posted today on the town green," Colonel Whiting cried aloud to his men. "It orders us to swear allegiance to the King and to abandon our *delusion* of independence. It further states that if we lay down our arms and return peacefully to our homes, that no harm will come to us or our property." Colonel Whiting paused. "Well, what say you, men? Shall we all go home and give up the fight?" The men erupted. Fists were raised in anger, muskets and swords were brandished defiantly. Passionate words of loyalty and dedication were shouted back in answer. Smiling, Colonel Whiting dropped the dispatch to the ground. "Follow me," he said to Reverend Sayre. He turned and strode away, stepping onto the dispatch with a heavy boot.

Colonel Whiting penned his answer to General Tryon. He wrote, "Connecticut has nobly dared to take up arms against the cruel despotism of Britain, and as the flames have now preceded your flag, they will persist to oppose to the utmost that power worked against injured innocence." He folded the paper and handed it to the reverend. "Deliver *this* to your general, Reverend Sayre."

Chapter Twelve

 The Pillaging of Fairfield

General Tryon's mouth became a thin line as anger hardened his visage. He tossed Colonel Whiting's answer back at Reverend Sayre. "So, the rebel traitors have decided to lose their town in their futile fight for independence! Well, then. So be it!" Tryon turned to his officer and ordered more buildings burned. Reverend Sayre looked aghast. He pleaded with the general. "General Tryon, do not do this, I beg of you. These people are good people. I have lived among them these many years. Do not destroy their homes and their livelihoods, I pray you..." Tryon turned impatiently to Reverend Sayre. "Your good people are traitors, Reverend Sayre." The reverend nodded in sad agreement. "They are misguided, General. They listen to leaders greedy for power and opportunity. They do not understand the folly and consequences of independence from Britain. They even imprisoned me for a time because of my loyalty to Britain and the King, but I have been attempting to reach them..."

"And you have failed, sir."

"General, there are a small number of loyalists in town. What of their houses? What of the churches and the homes of the ministers? What of the meetinghouse? The school? Are they all to be burned?" General Tryon sighed impatiently and thought for a moment. He called over one of his officers and spoke quietly to him. "I will write orders of protection for the buildings you have mentioned. Accompany me to Mrs. Buckley's. I will need the names of the loyalists." Tryon strode across the green. Reverend Sayre followed obediently behind.

After Reverend Sayre hurriedly departed the Buckley house clutching the orders of protection, General Tryon ordered the burnings of a larger number of buildings. His remaining troops on the green divided into groups to accomplish the deed. The sun was low in the sky and shadows stretched long across the road as soldiers escorted the blazing torches to buildings and homes selected by Tryon and Garth for destruction. The two generals strode about town directing their men. Flames and smoke appeared all over town. The sound of timbers snapping and falling, women screaming and men shouting filled the air. From the outskirts of town where Tryon had set up outposts came the sound of musket fire and cannon. The militia was trying to penetrate the British defenses. From far off came the rumble of thunder. It seemed that even nature intended to add to the furor of the evening.

A few brave town folk had remained in town hidden in their homes. As bands of soldiers approached their houses, they shot at them from windows. Several British fell in the road. The enraged soldiers hunted down the snipers. They bayoneted them or shot them in the chest as they attempted to flee.

Friedrich and Karl were attached to a group heading toward the west end of town. They were enjoying their mission. They had plundered several homes before putting them to the torch. They had emptied drawers and cupboards looking for valuables, small and easy to carry. They had smashed fine china and porcelain, broken windows, kicked at furniture and slashed fabrics and quilts. They helped themselves to food and drink as they went, and when they were satisfied they set the house ablaze and moved on.

At one home a woman stood defiantly in her doorway displaying a letter of protection signed by General Tryon. Friedrich and Karl looked at each other, nodded and turned as if to leave. The woman sank relieved against the doorframe. But the two Hessians burst out laughing and turned back toward the woman. Friedrich snatched the order from her and tore it to shreds. He ripped a pendant from her throat and pulled a ring roughly from her finger as she struggled and cried out. The two pushed past her and quickly searched the rooms for valuables as she stood weeping and pleading in the doorway. They set the house afire and shoved past her, laughing as they came back out. The woman rushed inside. She grabbed a heavy rug and beat desperately at the flames. The futility of the effort though, soon became apparent to her. Fires had been set all over the house. The blaze had taken hold and the heat and smoke became too much for her. She ran out of the house choking and sobbing and lay in a crumpled heap as her home burned away behind her.

Raiding parties were busy at their work all along the road. They were running from house to house, destroying, pillaging and insulting any town folk, mostly women, who got in their way. They cheered and congratulated each other when the houses burst into flame. Pouches bulged with coins, jewelry, silver buckles and other trinkets. Tryon and Garth did their best to maintain order and discipline amongst the troops and to treat the inhabitants with as much humanity as possible, considering the nature of their errand. However, they could not oversee every location in town.

Friedrich and Karl were in high spirits as they approached Sarah Middleton's house. The modest colonial stood proudly silhouetted against the pink-streaked sky. A barn and outbuildings were behind it to the right, and the cornfield, herb garden and vegetable crops behind to the left. Friedrich smiled. "This is a prosperous looking homestead, Karl."

"It is indeed," Karl replied. The two hurried up the path to the front door. Karl pushed down on the door latch and found that the door had been locked against them. "Someone is at home," said Karl. He handed his torch to Friedrich and stepped back from the door. He raised his foot and kicked hard several times just below the door handle. Wood cracked and splintered and the door flew open. Friedrich and Karl rushed inside but froze suddenly in their tracks. Sarah Middleton was standing in the center hall with a musket pointed at them. "Do not come a step closer!" she said. Friedrich glanced at Karl and spoke briefly to him in German. "I will throw the torch behind her. While she is distracted, grab the musket." Sarah did not understand the German words but she was very uneasy. "Go!" she shouted. "Go. Get out! I will shoot if I have to. Do you understand me? I will shoot!" Suddenly, Friedrich tossed the flaming torch behind Sarah, where it landed in an open doorway leading to the front parlor. Sarah jumped and swung around instinctively as the flaming torch flew through the air. Karl stepped forward, grabbed hold of the musket barrel and wrenched it from Sarah's hands. Sarah gasped and stepped back from Karl, who was smiling and aiming the musket directly at Sarah's breast. "No!" she gasped. She glanced behind her and saw that the flames were licking up the door frame with astonishing speed. She turned back to the Hessians and pleaded desperately. "No, please, do not do this." Her face was white with shock and horror. Friedrich smiled at her cruelly. "Guard her well, Karl," he said in German again. "This one has spirit!"

Friedrich ran up the stairs and quickly jerked open drawers in all the rooms. He rummaged through the contents and tossed them with disgust onto the floor. He threw open chests and emptied them. He thumped down the stairs and searched the rooms downstairs. He found nothing of any value. He became very agitated. Friedrich stepped toward Sarah and roughly grasped her shoulder. In heavily accented English he said, "The money, the jewelry...where is it?" Sarah looked up into Friedrich's face. He glared at her, waiting for her answer with hard, cold eyes. She knew that the house was lost. It would burn down just like so many others in town already had. Anger bubbled up in her. Her face distorted into a sneer. *"Find it!"* She said. Friedrich sputtered in anger. He dug his fingers cruelly into Sarah's shoulder and shoved her into the wall. He brought his face close to hers and with tightly clenched teeth he snarled at her. *"Foolish woman!"* He turned to Karl. "I'm going to have another look around. There's not much time. Take her outside. See if you can persuade her to talk." Karl grabbed hold of Sarah. Friedrich spun around and dashed up the stairs. The fire was taking hold and spreading rapidly. Karl grinned into Sarah's face. "We had better get outside, don't you think?" He pulled Sarah roughly toward the back of the house, through the kitchen and out of the door into the yard. "Now," he said. "Where have you hidden your little treasure, eh? Tell me!" Sarah stood calmly defiant and said nothing. Karl growled in anger. "Tell me or I will drag you back inside and let you burn with your house." Sarah gasped and retreated a step. Karl lunged forward and grasped Sarah by her shoulders. He shook her roughly. "Tell me, I say. Tell me." When Sarah still did not respond, Karl pushed her violently from him. Sarah lurched backwards and fell hard on the ground. Her head struck the tree stump where the family chopped their firewood. She lay stunned and groaning.

Ben burst out of the cornfield with a wild yelp and charged toward Karl. He held the axe above his head with the intention of plunging it into Karl's skull. Karl spun around taken aback by the outburst. He swung his musket from his shoulder. He did not have the time to load it but the bayonet would serve him just as well. He smiled in amusement as the boy ran toward him. When Ben was within ten feet, a musket cracked. Karl staggered and fell. Ben watched as a bright red stain appeared and spread over the front of the Hessian's shirt. Karl was on his back gasping for breath, staring up at the sky. Ben spun in the direction of the shot and saw Thomas standing in the long grass beside the barn. Thomas started to run toward Ben and his mother. "Thomas! Thomas!" Ben cried. "There's another one inside!" At that moment, Friedrich appeared in the doorway. His eyes swept over the scene in astonishment. His gaze rested on Karl. He was bloody and panting on the ground. *"Karl!"* he cried in dismay. *"Karl!"* Friedrich cocked his weapon and brought it swiftly to his shoulder. He took careful aim. Ben was standing in the middle of the yard still clutching his axe. He turned his head toward the door just as Friedrich pulled the trigger. *"Thomas!"* he screamed as the musket cracked. Thomas staggered sideways and dropped his musket. He exhaled heavily with the impact of the musket ball. His hand flew to his shoulder. He stumbled and fell into the long grass. Friedrich smiled with satisfaction and then ran to Karl. Ben dropped his axe and stared in horror. He rushed to his mother's side. "Mama...Mama," he cried. "Are you alright?" Sarah groaned in response. Ben looked over toward where his brother had fallen. Thomas was struggling to his feet. Ben had to help him, but how could he leave his mother? He looked around in desperation and with huge relief saw two women hurrying toward them. Ellen Jarvis and Elizabeth Cutler had come to check on Sarah. As they approached the house, they realized that a fire had been started. When they heard the musket fire they had become even more alarmed. They saw Sarah lying on the ground. The women glanced nervously at the Hessian soldier who was bending intently over his comrade, and then ran to Sarah's side to assess her condition. Ben stood up. "Please, take care of her," he beseeched them. "I've got to go to Thomas. He's been shot." He turned and dashed away without waiting for a reply.

Friedrich knelt beside Karl and fought back tears. He examined the wound and knew his friend would not survive. Karl was trembling. Blood was seeping from the corner of his mouth. He was panting in quick, short breaths, but his eyes focused on Friedrich, who was bending over him in despair. Friedrich watched his friend die. He spoke soothingly and reassuringly to him. "It will be alright, Karl," he said with great effort to keep his voice steady. "Just rest a while now. We'll be going home soon. You are going to build a big fine house..." Karl smiled into Friedrich's eyes. "Home," he breathed hoarsely. "Yes, Friedrich, a fine house...a wife...children. It's time..." Friedrich lifted his head, struggling to keep his emotions in check. He saw Ben and Thomas disappear into the cornfield. He turned back to Karl. Karl reached blindly for Friedrich. "Talk to me. Talk to me, Friedrich. Tell me about my house...tell me about the family I will have."

"It will be a big house, Karl..." Friedrich answered rather hoarsely. "...Big enough for lots of children. You will have much fine land and many fine cows and sheep and..." Karl's grip tightened on Friedrich's hand. He took two more short, gasping breaths and then his head fell to the side. His eyes were staring. His smile fixed. Friedrich stayed with Karl a moment longer, gazing tormented at his dead friend's face. He bowed his head and whispered a prayer in German.

He stood and reloaded his musket. *"I will avenge you!"* he said in parting to Karl. The Middleton house was well ablaze now. Fire hissed and crackled as timbers broke and crashed down. Smoke rose and drifted lazily across the cornfield.

Friedrich walked over to the women who were helping a groggy Sarah get to her feet. He looked directly into Sarah's face. *"Foolish woman,"* he sneered. "Watch your house burn! Your entire town will be gone by morning!" Ellen and Elizabeth guided Sarah away. They slowly walked away from the blaze and toward the road. Sarah was weeping. Friedrich headed toward the cornfield.

Chapter Thirteen

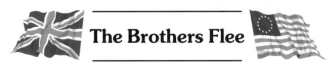

The Brothers Flee

Thomas knew they were in great danger. As he and Ben emerged from the far side of the cornfield he could feel blood dripping through his fingers. He needed help quickly. Ben looked nervously at his brother. The front of his shirt was soaked with blood. He took charge. "Come on, Thomas," he said. "Come with me." He grabbed hold of Thomas's arm and guided him at a faltering half-run across the field toward the creek.

At the creek's edge Thomas sat gratefully in the grass, resting his back against the trunk of the old oak tree. The trunk was broad. Strong gnarly branches spread wide above his head. The boys were in the shadow but the top of the tree caught the glow of the sunset. The eastern sky, though, was becoming dark. An ominous line of heavy clouds threatened on the horizon and far off thunder rumbled from time to time, adding nature's angry voice to the violent sounds of war.

Thomas looked down at his shirt and ripped it open. He twisted his neck to examine his shoulder.

The wound was puffy and raw. A steady, continuous leakage of blood oozed from the mutilated flesh. Ben dropped to his knees beside his brother and gazed anxiously at the wound. "We've got to get to Aunt Mary's, Thomas. Do you think you can make it?"

"I think so, Ben," Thomas nodded. "But we've got to do something about this shoulder first. I need something to press against the wound to slow the bleeding." Ben jumped to his feet and began pulling at his shirt. "No, Ben, wait," said Thomas. "Open my pouch." Ben dropped to his knees again and fumbled with the buckle on the leather bag. He opened it and peered inside. He looked up into Thomas's face. "The flag," he said simply. Thomas smiled weakly and nodded. Ben withdrew the flag. It was neatly folded. "Fold it twice more, Ben, and give it to me." Ben obeyed and handed it to his brother. Thomas placed it on top of the wound with a slight grimace. "*Now* your shirt. Wrap it around my shoulder. Tie it with the sleeves, Ben...as tight as you can." Ben followed Thomas's instructions, hesitating when Thomas flinched and caught his breath. "No, Ben. It's alright. You are doing fine. Tie it tight now." When Ben was finished he helped Thomas to his feet. Thomas was pale and sweating. He led him to the water. They both drank quickly. "Come on, Thomas," said Ben. "We've got to hurry. That Hessian may be looking for us." Thomas nodded. He followed Ben across the creek and into the wooded field on the other side.

Friedrich searched through the cornfield. He had fixed his bayonet to the musket barrel and impatiently pushed back the cornstalks with it as he looked for the young rebel and the boy. Karl, his friend, was dead. Friedrich was consumed with rage and revenge. He would run them both through with his bayonet without a second thought when he found them. And he *would* find them. He had shot the young rebel. He could not go far. Friedrich emerged from the cornfield. They were not there. He looked around, scanning the landscape in all directions. There was no sign of them. Friedrich studied the ground, walking the perimeter of the cornfield. He stopped. His mouth curled in a sardonic grin. On the ground were drops of fresh blood. He followed their trail.

Chapter Fourteen

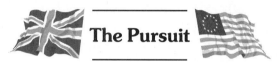

The Pursuit

Ben had traveled the distance to Aunt Mary's countless times before. He had jogged through the woods and fields quickly and easily. In less than an hour, he could make it there and back. This evening, though, the farm seemed very far away. Thomas was making a heroic effort. Ben led the way. He knew the best trail with the smoothest ground for Thomas. He warned him of roots and rocks and holes and held back tree branches and brambles as they went. Thomas hurried after Ben as fast as he could. For a while they made good progress. But as they cleared the woods and faced an open field again, Thomas stopped. He was perspiring and panting heavily. "I need to rest for just a moment, Ben," he said with a grimace as he leaned against a tree trunk. Ben stopped, swung around and hurried back to his brother. Thomas's face was pale and pinched with pain. Ben put his hand on Thomas's arm. "It's alright, Thomas. Just catch your breath. We'll soon be there. It'll be alright." Thomas managed a weak smile and closed his eyes.

Friedrich followed the blood trail to the creek, but there the trail ended. He searched in all directions.

He found no more blood. He waded across the creek to the woods. He scouted the area quickly until he found a narrow trail. He followed it. The woods were quite dim now. The bright light of day had gone and the glow of the sunset only touched the tips of the trees. He had to hurry. He had to find them before dark.

Thomas's eyes flew open. From deep in the woods he heard a dead branch snap. Ben inhaled sharply. Thomas put his finger to his lips and whispered, "Listen, Ben. Listen." They waited, nervous and tense, their ears straining for another sound. Very faintly, they heard the rustling of undergrowth. "Deer?" whispered Ben optimistically. Thomas shook his head. *"The Hessian."* Thomas scanned the field quickly. "To the rocks, Ben. Hurry!" But Ben shook his head. "That's where he will go. Come on, Thomas, this way," Ben commanded, pulling at Thomas's sleeve. Thomas put a hand on Ben's shoulder and leaned on him as they made their way across the field to a grassy knoll. They lay down behind the little mound and peered through the long grass toward the woods. The Hessian emerged. He strode several paces into the clearing and scanned the terrain. Pastureland, lush and green even in the diminishing light. The land sloped away from the woods in a slow decline. To his left a hundred strides away was an outcropping of jagged rocks, to his right, hilly, uneven land. Further below on the right, several hundred strides away, was a low hedge bordering another field. Friedrich searched for signs of blood. He found none. He could see no sign of the rebels. He did not think they were far enough ahead of him to have made it all the way to the hedge.

They had to be hiding amongst the rocks. He strode off toward them.

Ben and Thomas watched the Hessian turn in the wrong direction. They waited a moment and then hastened down the hillside, crouching low to the ground. The slope and hillocks kept them hidden from view most of the time. Thomas staggered clumsily as they made their way. Several times he reached out and grabbed Ben's arm to prevent himself from falling. He was becoming weak and weary and his wound throbbed painfully. They made it to the hedge. Ben crawled through. A low moan escaped from Thomas as he dragged himself through the small opening. Ben grasped his uninjured arm and helped him to his feet. "Come on, Thomas," Ben urged cheerfully. "Let's get across this field. We'll soon be there." Ben led his brother as fast as he thought Thomas could manage. He felt Thomas leaning more heavily on him and was afraid he would collapse at any time. He glanced up at the sky. Overhead it was a dull gray. On the western horizon was a faint reddish glow where the sun had disappeared. Soon the Hessian would not be able to see them at all.

Friedrich was angry. He had been certain he would find the rebels hiding amongst the rocks. He had checked the perimeter and then climbed up onto them, peering down into the cracks and crevices. They were not there. They must have headed toward the hedge after all. Friedrich ran across the pasture, cursing in his native German. The twilight would soon fade to darkness. He did not have much time. He reached the hedge and searched impatiently for an opening. He shoved his way through and looked around wildly. On the far side of the field was a tangle of thicket. He saw two shadowy figures disappear behind it.

Ben spoke encouragingly to Thomas as they lumbered on. "Soon it will be dark and he won't be able to see us. He doesn't know the land, but we do, don't we, Thomas? Soon we will be safe, only a few more fields. We'll make it." Thomas could not answer. It was all he could do to keep putting one foot in front of the other. His good arm was slung around Ben's shoulder and he leaned heavily as he trudged forward, crossing field after field after field. He was relying on Ben to guide him. He had lost track of the way. He was lightheaded and exhausted. He stumbled on without thought, in a daze. "Be careful here, Thomas. It's the gully. Then there's just a small hill to climb and we should be able to see the farmhouse." Thomas clutched onto Ben as he staggered into the gully and climbed painfully up the other side and to the top of the hill. He lay down on the hilltop, breathing deeply, his eyes closed. "Ben...," he breathed. "Can't make it. You must...go on without me."

"No, Thomas. Look! See. It's the farmhouse. We're there. You can make it." Thomas slowly raised his head and looked into the gloom. In the distance he could make out the dark shape of the farmhouse, and through the windows, the warm glow of candlelight inside. Ben was tugging at him. "Come on, Thomas. Come on. Just a little way further. You can make it. Hold on to me. Come on. Get up. *Get up!*" Thomas struggled weakly to his feet. Ben put his arm around Thomas as his brother all but collapsed against him. He carried as much of Thomas's weight as he could and they plodded on. He fixed his eyes on the farmhouse. He knew the Hessian would not be far behind. They reached the door. Ben fell against it fumbling for the door handle. The door swung open and the two stumbled inside, with Ben calling urgently for his aunt.

Friedrich smiled with satisfaction and anticipation when he saw the two dark figures on the hilltop. He watched them blend together into one shape and then disappear as they descended the hill on the other side. He crossed the field at a faster pace. He would have them soon. He did not see the gully until he was tumbling into it. He fell heavily to the ground. His musket flew from his grasp. Friedrich scrambled angrily to his feet. As he stepped forward to retrieve the musket, a sharp pain in his ankle caused him to stumble. He had twisted it in the fall. He cursed, picked up his musket and limped on. He climbed out of the gully and up the hill with painful grunts and groans. He dusted himself off as he looked ahead into the dusk and then stopped suddenly. He stood motionless as his gaze rested on the farmhouse. So this was where they were headed, he thought to himself. There was no movement or sign of the two figures. Friedrich knew they must be inside. A slow smile spread across his face. Now it was going to be easy.

Chapter Fifteen

 The Hiding Place

Aunt Mary gasped with shock when she rushed into the hallway. It was dimly lit with candlelight but she could see that Thomas was seriously injured. He was pale and moaning with his eyes closed, and his shirt was ragged and bloody. Ben was trying to hold him up and was straining under the effort. "Oh, Thomas," she cried. "Oh, no!" She hurried forward to help him. "Aunt Mary," Ben panted. "Quick, lock the door! There is an enemy soldier following us."

Ned appeared in the hallway and then Abby and two of the children. Abby took one look at Thomas and froze. "Thomas!" she sobbed. Ned turned to face Abby. "Now, Abby," he said calmly. "It's going to be alright. You must take care of the children so that we can tend to Thomas. Go along now, Abby." Abby gulped back her sobs and struggled for control. Her face was crumpled in despair but she nodded obediently and hustled the children away.

Mary ran to the door, closed it and slid the bolt. "He's not far behind us. We've got to hide...quickly!" Ben declared. Ned strode swiftly over to Thomas. He

64

put an arm around Thomas's waist and draped the uninjured arm over his shoulders. "Now, my lad, lean on me," he said firmly. "I'll help you. We're going upstairs. Do you understand?" Thomas nodded weakly, eyes closed and half conscious. The old man, sturdy and strong from years of hard work on the farm, mounted the staircase half carrying Thomas. Ben picked up one of the candles burning on the hall table and followed closely behind. "I'm taking him to the attic, Mary. Get some water and clean cloths." Mary rushed to the kitchen and returned with a bowl of hot water taken from the kettle on the fire and some cloths draped over her arm. She hurried up the stairs. At the top of the stairs Ned continued down a long dark hallway until he reached a door at the end. "Open it, Ben," he commanded. Ben raised the candle and lifted the latch on the rough-hewn attic door. The stairs to the attic were narrow and steep and halfway up they turned to the left. Ned proceeded slowly and carefully so that he would not bump Thomas against the walls. The attic floor had wide wood planking, and rough boards formed walls, closing off the eaves on the sides. A few odd pieces of furniture, a rolled up carpet, a large wooden chest and an assortment of baskets were stored in the attic room.

Ned gently sat Thomas on the floor. He fitted his fingers into a groove in the wall on the right side of the attic space and removed a section of wallboard. He crouched to enter the opening and pulled Thomas inside. Ben crawled in after them. Mary placed the bowl and cloths inside the crawlspace and was about to follow when an ominous thudding and pounding could be heard downstairs. She could hear the children crying and Abby's panicked voice calling up the stairs, "Ned, Aunt Mary, someone is trying to break down the door!" Ned spoke urgently to Ben. "Stay here with your brother. Remove the bloody rags from the wound and clean it. Use these cloths to bandage it until we get back. Make him as comfortable as you can, Ben." He patted Ben firmly on the shoulder and crawled out. Ned replaced the wallboard and then turned his attention to Mary. "Now, Mary. Let us go see about our unexpected visitor." Mary stood up and smoothed her dress. She nodded at Ned, managed a quivering smile, and the two hurried downstairs.

A distraught Abby was in the hall holding one of the children. Two others clutched at her skirts, crying. Ned and Mary had just made it to the bottom of the stairs and were turning to console them when Friedrich burst in. The bolt gave way and the door flew open. Ned stepped forward to block his way but Friedrich pushed him roughly aside. He limped brazenly past Mary, Abby and the children and searched each of the downstairs rooms, holding his bayoneted musket menacingly before him. He returned to the hallway and approached Mary. *"Where are they?"* he demanded. Mary took a step back. "Who are you looking for?" she asked. Friedrich's eyes narrowed. *"They are here. I know they are here. Where are they?"* Mary shook her head. "There's only us..." Friedrich looked around at the pathetic family group and sneered. "Ignorant peasants!" he said. "I will find them." His eyes rested on Abby. "You...girl, get a candle and lead the way upstairs!" Abby stepped back, her eyes wide with fear. She looked desperately at Ned. "Do as he says,

Abby," Ned told her gently. Abby took a deep, shaky breath and handed the small child she was holding to Mary. Ned took the hands of the two other children. Abby picked up a candle from the hall table and slowly mounted the stairs. Friedrich followed.

Friedrich directed Abby to enter the two rooms at the top of the stairs. He searched quickly stabbing at furniture and bedding with his bayonet. He opened chests and wardrobes and stabbed at the clothing and linens inside. He looked under beds and behind doors. He followed Abby down the long hall and searched the front two bedrooms. Then Friedrich noticed the attic door. "Open this door, girl!" he demanded. Abby complied. She climbed the steps and waited. Friedrich was slower on the attic steps. The steepness of the stairs aggravated his sprained ankle. He grunted as he climbed. Abby kept her eyes on the floor, not daring to look at the man. The look of cruelty and determination on his face shook her to the bone. She frowned. She noticed something on the floor beside her next to the wall. With sickening certainty, she knew what it was, blood, Thomas's blood. She moved slowly to her right, concealing it beneath her skirts. Friedrich barged past her. He emptied the chest and stabbed at the carpet in his fury. Abby prayed that he would not investigate further. He walked towards her suddenly and took the candle from her hands. He walked around the attic room, looking at the walls and floorboards. Abby held her breath. Friedrich sputtered in frustration. He returned to the stairs, thrust the candle at Abby and began his painful climb down. Abby slowly released her breath and followed him.

Ben had been holding his breath too when he heard the noise on the other side of the attic wall. He knew it was the Hessian. He huddled over the candle, blocking any light that might show through joints or holes in the wallboard. Thomas was in a fitful sleep but he made no sound. Ben had already removed the shirt and the folded flag that had been placed over Thomas's wound. The flag was wet and heavy with blood. He had put it beside Thomas on the floor. Ben had then cleaned around the ravaged area very carefully with hot water and a clean cloth. Then he had folded a fresh bandage and gently pressed it onto Thomas's shoulder. It was then that he heard Friedrich and Abby on the stairs. He stopped and waited, watching his brother nervously. He listened intently. For several minutes he heard the scuffling of boots on the floorboards and scraping and thudding. He heard the boots walk the perimeter of the room and feared that the Hessian would decide to pry away at the wallboard. But then, with relief, he heard the sound of footsteps descending the stairs. Ben took a deep breath and dipped a cloth into the water to wash away more blood.

Abby led Friedrich back downstairs to the hallway where Mary waited anxiously with Ned and the children. Friedrich grabbed Ned's arm roughly and gave him a wicked grin. "Let's have a look in your barn." He took down a lantern hanging on a hook by the door and handed it to Ned. He turned to Abby. "Light it, girl!" Abby stepped toward him and lit the lantern with her candle. Friedrich shoved Ned forward and through the open doorway. "Lead the way, old man," he commanded. Ned stumbled out of the house. He crossed the dusty yard filled with apprehension. Friedrich followed close behind him with his bayonet pointed at his back.

The smell of smoke was strong in the air and Ned noticed a distinct glow on the horizon in the direction of town. Lightning flashed and thunder still rumbled from time to time as a storm threatened. Ned had never known such a night. He reached the barn and stopped. "Open the doors!" Friedrich demanded. Ned lifted the wooden bar from the iron hasp and the heavy doors swung open towards him. The Hessian grabbed the lantern from Ned's grasp and entered the barn, holding the lantern high. He surveyed the interior quickly. There were several stalls containing two horses and a few cows. Leather straps and bridles hung on hooks from the timbers. Tools leaned against the barn walls. There were large mounds of hay. Friedrich peered into each stall. Finding no sign of his prey, he hung the lantern on a hook and with the wild expression of a madman began stabbing savagely at the hay with his bayonet. He snarled in German through gritted teeth as he attacked the hay and finally exploded in fury when he found no one hiding there.

Friedrich reached for the lantern and roared. *"They are here...I know they are here!"* His eyes frantically darted around the barn again. He noticed a crudely made ladder leading to the hayloft. He stared at it and then a slow smile spread across his face. He tossed the lantern into the hay. The hay caught fire. Ned reacted immediately. He rushed to the stalls and released the horses and cows. He whooped and slapped them smartly on the rump, chasing them out of the barn. Friedrich laughed. The flames leapt up, spreading rapidly. He stood in the barn and watched for a moment, relishing the devastation he had set in motion. Still chuckling with satisfaction he limped out of the barn to a safe distance in the shadows. He loaded his musket ready to fire at Karl's killers when they tried to escape.

Mary and the children were watching from the doorway. Mary inhaled sharply when she saw the fire. "Stay here," she said to Abby. She ran across the yard to the well. She dropped the bucket in and began cranking ferociously on the handle. She felt a touch on her shoulder. She jumped and turned. It was Ned. "Don't," he said softly. "There's no use, Mary." She looked at Ned and then at the barn. The fire was expanding at a frightening pace. One side of the barn was well ablaze. The old dry timbers and boards succumbed easily. She nodded meekly. Ned put an arm around her and guided her back to the house. "Stay here," he said. He turned back to the yard and headed toward the woodpile.

In the attic, Ben heard the commotion outside. He pushed at the wallboard and crawled out. There was light coming in through the small attic window at the top of the stairs. Ben hurried to it and peered outside. The barn was on fire! It was the Hessian. He was burning the barn. He would burn the house next. *"No!"* he cried aloud. Abby, Mary, Ned and the children were all in terrible danger. Ben sprang from the window and dashed down the stairs. He was responsible for this, he thought. It was his fault. He had brought this on them all.

Thomas stirred in the attic space. His shoulder burned and throbbed painfully. He opened his eyes and slowly looked around. He did not know where he was. In the dim light of the candle he could make out the wooden wall beside him and the rough-hewn roof rafters sloping above him. He felt weak and feverish. He lay back and closed his eyes. He tried to think but his mind was fuzzy. He frowned trying to remember. He was running with Ben across the fields. They were going to the farmhouse...to Aunt Mary's. He felt pain, such pain in his shoulder. Shot...he had been shot. He remembered. The Hessian soldier...following. Ben... Abby...Aunt Mary... Where were they? he wondered. Danger...great danger. Thomas opened his eyes. He had to help them. He rolled onto his side and tried to get to his knees, but his heart pounded and his head reeled with the effort. He lacked the strength. He slumped back on the floorboards, breathing heavily. He stared helplessly at the opening in the wall. It seemed to be a little brighter. There was light coming in through the window. Perhaps it was morning, he thought. In the candlelight and the added glow from the window, Thomas noticed a familiar folded cloth lying on the floor beside him. He picked it up and brought it closer to his face. It was the flag...Papa's flag. He remembered...they had used it as a bandage and it was wet and heavy with his blood. Tears sprang to Thomas's eyes. This flag was so precious. His father had entrusted it to him. It was the symbol for which they fought. He had to keep it safe for Papa. He had to protect it. If the Hessian should find him...

Thomas moved his head slowly from side to side, scanning the small space. He studied the rafters above him. He must be in the eave just under the roof. He laid the flag on the floor, twisted onto his hip and reached up with his good arm. The pounding in his head intensified. His shoulder throbbed and he felt blood trickling down his chest. Thomas ran his hand along one of the rafters. His fingers found a space between the rafter and the boards of the roof. He picked up the flag and pushed it into the space. He made sure that it was all tucked out of sight before he let his arm drop. He lay back. "The flag is safe, Papa," he whispered aloud. He closed his eyes as exhaustion overcame him.

Ben ran into the kitchen and looked around desperately. He grabbed a carving knife from the cutting board and a large, pewter candlestick from the table. If he could catch the Hessian by surprise, he thought...Ben glanced down the hallway toward the open door. His aunt, Abby and the children stood in the yard just outside. They had their backs to him and were staring hopelessly toward the flaming barn. Ben returned to the kitchen and left the house by the back door. He walked around the back and along the side of the house until he could peer around the corner and look into the yard. He looked beyond the little group huddled by the door. He looked for the Hessian. The fire was roaring as flames greedily devoured the barn. Long shadows were cast across the yard. He studied the shadows carefully. His gaze shifted to a shape barely visible in the darkness to the side of the barn. It was a crouching figure. It had to be the Hessian. Ben could make out the musket he was holding. He quickly formulated a plan. He would go back behind the house and then move in a wide circle around the perimeter of the yard, staying in the darkness. He would sneak up behind the Hessian and smack him as hard as he could on the head with the candlestick. He looked down at the knife uncertainly. He would take it with him. He hoped he would not have to use it.

Ben crouched low as he made his way around the yard. He advanced silently and stayed deep in the shadows. He kept his eyes fastened on the yard and prayed that the Hessian would not move from his position into the light. When he was directly behind the dark figure, Ben stopped. He was about twenty paces away. His heart was beating rapidly. He took a deep breath to calm his nerves. Tightening his grip on the candlestick, he advanced toward the Hessian. He was more than halfway toward him when his foot kicked a loose stone. The stone skipped and rolled rapidly across the hard dirt yard. It rolled past Friedrich and stopped several paces ahead of him. Ben froze. Friedrich's head jerked and then he was on his feet and spinning around. He stood staring at Ben in stunned surprise for a moment. His gaze fell to the knife and candlestick in Ben's hands and then a slow, cruel smile spread across his face. He raised his musket and positioned it against his shoulder. He stared down the barrel, aiming at the center of Ben's chest. "Good-bye, peasant boy!" he said.

Friedrich's shot went wild. Just before he pulled the trigger he lurched forward. The musket ball missed Ben several paces to the left. A hatchet protruded from Friedrich's back. Old Ned stood beside the woodpile in the yard from where he had thrown it. Friedrich turned and looked at him in stunned disbelief. "I was always good with a hatchet," Ned said simply. Friedrich made desperate, futile attempts to reach the hatchet. He reeled and stumbled in his efforts. He staggered wildly around the barnyard while the others looked on in horror. Friedrich teetered out of control toward the barn and fell through the doorway. He disappeared into the flames.

Chapter Sixteen

 ## The Smoldering Remains

The following morning Ben left the farm at dawn. He was worried about Thomas. They had moved him from the attic into a bed. Aunt Mary had tried to remove the musket ball but it had penetrated very deeply and she was afraid of probing too much and causing more blood loss. Thomas had been restless and delirious during the night. Ben had a sickening fear in the pit of his stomach. He had to get to town and find Dr. Gordon. He also had to find his mother. He was worried about her too. He prayed that she was safe.

Ben glanced at the remains of the barn as he ran past. It was a smoldering heap of scorched timbers. He shivered as he thought of the enemy soldier whose burnt remains lay amongst the ashes and ruins that he himself had wrought. It was a fitting end, but horrendous nonetheless. Ben ran swiftly across the fields where so recently he had struggled with his brother. The smell of smoke hung heavy in the air as he approached Fairfield. He dashed through the woods and then through the cornfield that lay just beyond. He brushed past the last of the cornstalks and stood in his yard. His house was in ruin. The chimney still stood, and several scorched upright timbers. The rest was a pile of blackened rubble. From deep within, embers glowed and smoke trailed up and drifted lazily into the air. The sight of his home, destroyed, lost, smoldering there before him in an untidy heap brought Ben to tears. He sat down heavily and stared at it and sobbed.

After a while Ben wiped away his tears with the sleeve of his shirt. It was too big, one of Uncle Matthew's that Aunt Mary had given him to wear. The barn was still there and looked to be undamaged. He wondered if his mother might be inside, but he did not want to cross the yard. The Hessian soldier's body still lay on the ground. He called out, "Mama! Mama, are you there?" He called again, louder, *"Mama!"* He waited. There was no answer. Ben slowly got to his feet and walked to the road. He headed toward the center of town. He looked around in shock and amazement. The devastation in Fairfield was overwhelming. Burning parties were still at their work. Ben heard shouts in the distance and saw the flames of new fires in all directions. From time to time he heard the crack of muskets from British outposts around the town. A blue haze hung in the air. Ben passed mound after mound of smoking debris where the homes of friends and neighbors had so recently stood. He stopped in the road and stared at the plot where Dr. Gordon's house had been. It had been a grand house. Two fireplaces and part of the chimneys stood amid the wreckage. Dr. Gordon's dog lay in front of the heap, his head resting on his paws.

The dog glanced up for a moment and gave Ben a forlorn look, then lowered his head again.

As Ben neared the center of town he came upon several homes still standing. Several town folk stood around. Their faces were tense and strained. Some of them clutched papers in their hands. An elderly man and a woman struggled as they lifted a body out of the road. Ben followed them in morbid fascination as they carried the corpse to the churchyard and laid it gently on the grass. There were several other bodies already lying there. As they left the churchyard, they saw Ben. The old man looked down at Ben with a grim expression. "All brave souls, Ben," he said, sadly shaking his head. Ben nodded absently still mesmerized by the familiar faces of town folk and militiamen lying before him. "Come on, lad," the old man continued, placing a hand on Ben's shoulder. "Away from here now. You should not be in town. What are you..." Ben jerked around suddenly. "Mrs. Lewis, I'm looking for my mother. Have you seen her?" The woman answered him. "She is at the Jarvis house, lad. General Tryon spared her house in return for her agreeing to nurse a wounded British officer. Most of the women who were burned out of their homes are there."

"Thank you," Ben said quickly. He turned and ran to the Jarvis house. He knocked urgently on the door. A woman opened it. "Mrs. Cutler, is my mama here?" Ben asked breathlessly. "Oh Ben! Yes, yes, she is here! Come in." She hurried into the house. "Sarah! It's Ben. Ben's here." Sarah suddenly appeared in the hallway. Ben stood just inside the door. "Ben!" she cried. Ben flew into her arms. "Mama, Mama.

Are you alright? That soldier hurt you. I was so worried."

"I'm alright, Ben. Don't worry about me." She bent down and held Ben by the shoulders and looked directly into his eyes. "Thomas," she said. "Ellen Jarvis told me he was shot. How is he, Ben?" Ben's eyes filled with tears. "He's very weak, Mama. I got him to Aunt Mary's, but he lost a lot of blood. The Hessian...he followed us. Mama, we need Dr. Gordon...his house is burned...Thomas needs him." Sarah stood up slowly and hugged Ben to her. "Oh, no," she whispered. She turned desperately to the small group of women standing pityingly behind her. Ellen Jarvis moved forward and laid a hand on her shoulder. "We'll do our best to find Dr. Gordon and get him out to the farm. You go with Ben. Take care of Thomas until he gets there." Sarah nodded thankfully and gave Ellen a quick hug. She smiled bravely at the others and then hurried with Ben down the dusty road in the direction of her sister's farm.

The enemy was encamped on the town green. General Tryon and General Garth departed the Buckley house for the last time. Mrs. Jonathan Buckley watched them leave. Her house was safe but Fairfield was changed forever. She knew that soon she would have to face her neighbors and fellow town folk and learn the full extent of the devastation wrought by the British. Most of them would hate her for what she had done. "Foolish, stubborn people," she thought. They were so obsessed with the right to be free and so determined to be a separate country. They fought to be independent from Britain, the greatest, most powerful nation on earth. Mrs. Buckley sighed deeply. Flames and smoke rose from several locations as she stood on the step at the front of her house. She listened to cannon fire and muskets cracking as skirmishes continued on the outskirts of town. "Such folly. So much loss. So much pain and misery," she lamented. She shook her head sadly as she stepped back inside her house and closed the door.

General Tryon ordered retreat and the bugle blared. Burning parties returned to the green and made preparations to depart. Injured British soldiers were placed on carts to be transported to the ships. Officers took charge of their men, and in orderly formation the British troops began to march back toward the beach and the ships waiting at sea. A rear guard of mostly Hessian soldiers would remain behind for a while to ensure the safety of the departing troops. Scurrying along with the British were Reverend Sayre and his family. General Tryon had granted permission for them to leave Fairfield aboard the British ships.

General Tryon had spared the meetinghouse and churches and several homes with his letters of protection. The rear guard, however, had not had their fill of desecration. They laughed at the desperate women when they presented their orders of protection. They tore up the papers and barged into their homes, grabbing any valuables. They set fire to most of the remaining buildings as they pillaged and burned their way to the shoreline.

The militia pursued the departing troops. Colonel Whiting and his men ran down from Round Hill and through the smoky ruins of Fairfield. They followed them all the way to the point of embarkation. There were more losses on both sides during this final skirmish, but at noon the last of the enemy pushed away from shore in flatboats. Two hours later, the ships set sail, heading toward Long Island.

Chapter Seventeen

 A Patriot's Sacrifice

Thomas died three days later. Dr. Gordon managed to get to the farm late in the afternoon of the day that the enemy troops departed Fairfield. He did what he could for Thomas but his patient was too weak to fight the infection and fever that had set in so rapidly. Thomas never regained full consciousness, although he did open his eyes and smile at his mother when she arrived at his bedside. Sarah comforted her son, singing to him songs that he had heard as a baby. She spoke to him lovingly, praising him for his bravery, and assured him that he soon would be well. She did not leave his side until he drew his last shallow breath, and only then did she collapse into inconsolable sobs.

Two days later Ben stood pale and grief stricken, holding Abby's hand while she wept at Thomas's burial. Reverend Elliot conducted a service in the churchyard at the gravesite. Both churches in town had been burned to the ground. Many townsfolk were there. They came together to offer comfort and support to Sarah and the children and to each other. All had suffered great loss. There were many fresh graves in Fairfield.

The militia had continued to grow. Major Talmage from White Plains arrived with his army the day after the British had left. If the British had remained just one day longer, the outcome would have been very different. Major Talmage's men camped on the green. The desolate town folk were grateful for the protection and help of the troops. They bravely set about the business of reconstructing their homes and lives. Families temporarily adapted outbuildings or raised simple structures for shelter until they were able to erect permanent buildings. The British had hoped to crush the spirit of the people of Fairfield. However, they had only succeeded in reaffirming the determination of those people to be free of such a cruel and despicable foe.

The men on the green grew more and more incensed as the smoldering remains all about them reminded them of the atrocities of the enemy. Their feelings of anger and revenge were directed at Mrs. Buckley. The day after the British left Fairfield, a Captain Sturges positioned a field piece in front of her house. He threatened to demolish her house and anyone inside unless she left immediately. One hundred and fifty men supported him by standing around the cannon. It was a frightening episode. Someone got word to Colonel Whiting, who was on Holland Hill. He arrived promptly on the green and dispersed the men. "Has there not been enough death and destruction already?" he asked angrily. Of George Hoyt, there was no sign.

Sam and his family returned to town. Ben had little time to spend with Sam. Both boys worked very hard. There were animals to be cared for, crops to be tended, rubble to be cleared away and homes to be rebuilt. They went about their work stoically. Fairfield was their home. It would thrive again. With few exceptions the people of Fairfield stayed. A tremendous undertaking lay before them. But, they had survived the British assault. They had stood firm against the power and might of an oppressive enemy. They would rebuild. They would endure. They would become prosperous once again. The people of Fairfield rolled up their sleeves and got to work.

It was several weeks later when Sam asked Ben about Thomas's flag. Ben was startled. He had forgotten about it. He ran out to the farm and asked Aunt Mary if she had it. Aunt Mary was puzzled. She had not seen a flag when she cared for Thomas. She and Ben climbed the stairs to the attic. They looked behind the wall where Thomas had lain. They did not find the flag.

Epilogue

Fairfield sustained the following losses due to the raid by the British on July 7 and July 8, 1779:

83 houses
54 barns
47 shops and stores
2 schools
2 churches
1 jail
1 courthouse

Only six homes were left standing. The British left forty soldiers in shallow graves on the grounds of the meetinghouse. They were later moved to unmarked graves in the ancient cemetery. Ten Americans died.

House spared by the British

A house near the town green still stands on Beach Lane (now known as Beach Road).

Photograph by the author

Beach Lane

British troops marched from beach landing to the town center.

Photograph by the author

Inlet to Ash Creek

The militia prevented the British from crossing Ash Creek and attacking the fort at Grover's Hill.

Photograph by the author